Addison + Brooklyn,

May the spirit of
Christmas forever live in your hearts!.

XXOO

Amanda McL Hause

- 2019 -

Impish

The Christmas Elf

AMANDA MCILWAIN HAUSER

AuthorHouse™
1663 Liberty Drive
Bloomington, IN 47403
www.authorhouse.com
Phone: 1 (800) 839-8640

Because of the dynamic nature of the Internet, any web addresses or links contained in this book may have changed
since publication and may no longer be valid. The views expressed in this work are solely those of the author and do not
necessarily reflect the views of the publisher, and the publisher hereby disclaims any responsibility for them.

Any people depicted in stock imagery provided by Getty Images are models,
and such images are being used for illustrative purposes only.
Certain stock imagery © Getty Images.

This book is printed on acid-free paper.

ISBN: 978-1-7283-2179-0 (hc)
ISBN: 978-1-7283-2127-1 (sc)
ISBN: 978-1-7283-2128-8 (e)

Print information available on the last page.

Published by AuthorHouse 07/29/2019

authorHOUSE®

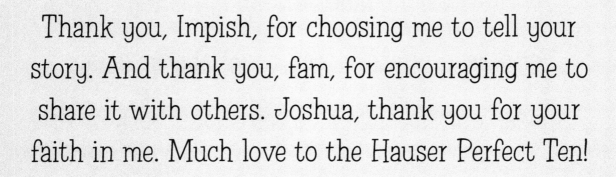

Thank you, Impish, for choosing me to tell your story. And thank you, fam, for encouraging me to share it with others. Joshua, thank you for your faith in me. Much love to the Hauser Perfect Ten!

All through the summer and into the spring,

Light dances and skips and glimmers and sings

Across the frozen tundra, where ice forever rests,

Where reindeer and polar bears are permanent guests.

Gently the light fades into long-lasting night,

For a deep winter's rest, to let the frost bite.

As bleak and desolate as a ten-thousand-foot hole,

Dark's a six-month-visitor at the North Pole.

For hundreds of years, Impish dreaded this black;

Cold and lifeless, it filled every crack.

And with it came sadness to this little elf,

For Impish found happiness in light itself.

But then one bleak night a thought popped in her head

As she shivered 'neath the covers in her tiny elf bed.

"If laughter is like light and giggles are warm,

I'll make my own rays, and sunshine will form

In the walls and the halls of this workshop so gray—

When I make a new game for the children to play!"

Like a snowflake she twirled and floated with glee

As she concocted her plans for under the tree!

It was just Impish's luck that her number one chore

In Santa's workshop so grand, behind the biggest door,

Was to size up each gift, then unroll, snip, and tape

Until each present shone in its papery cape

And was topped with a ribbon or sometimes a bow

And was labeled quite neatly with a name tag, just so.

She toiled in wrapping in her nimble elf way

Until Impish mixed things up that one fateful day.

"How boring are bows and paper and tags

When gifts could be pranks or tricks or gags!

That's how I'll do it! That's how I'll bring

The light to this darkness; I'll change everything!

No more plain ol' tags labeled 'From: Santa Claus.'

May his unopened gifts bring smiles because

They must first be matched to my tricky elfish clues!"

And she composed her plan without a minute to lose!

Her brain crafted so quickly, her hands couldn't keep pace,

And soon her first gimmick warmed the whole place!

"Into the stockings Santa will sneak

A one-of-kind ornament for each child to seek!

Hidden among toys and striped candy canes,

A gift of unique trimmings made on Santa Claus Lane."

No two treasures were the same, and
each a crafty elfish clue

Came from Impish herself and her
North Pole wrapping crew.

As the sun bubbled awake from its horizontal nap

And Christmas morning shed its glorious sleeping cap,

Under each tree, anxious hearts did seek,

Eager fingers trembled, and knees grew weak,

Sleepy-eyed children puzzled and stared

At Impish's handiwork placed carefully there.

Presents with no tags, no labels, no names—

Santa's impish elf playing Christmas games!

How could they decide which presents were whose?

How could they solve a sneaky wrapping-elf's clues?

Like brilliant white snow, young
minds solved the elf's plot,

Like detectives, the clues their clever eyes spot ...

Some gifts wrapped

Some wrapped in paper

Some gifts packaged

Some gifts hidden

in paper dotted with dolls...

checkered with balls,...

with silver bell crepe,...

within nutcracker paper and tape!

Popping and tumbling, thoughts
formed and thoughts hatched

In the brains of those children whose ornaments matched

Those Impishly crafted paper-wrapped gifts—

And born of that hope, the confusion did lift.

Can you guess it—this hint that's meant only for you?

Impish left inklings for you to solve too!

Match the tree ornament in your stocking stuffed tight

To the handmade elf paper 'neath the tree—what a sight!

With the help of little Impish and her sly elf ploys,

Santa left mysteries along with new toys!

Now in the inkiest of skies and blackest of days,

You'll find at the North Pole that Impish Elf plays.

For there's light from her games when
the days are not sunny,

And in the cold darkness is the birth of things funny!

Impish keeps busy with her pranks and her hoax,

For next Christmas she'll bring new antics and jokes!

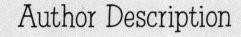

Author Description

Amanda McIlwain Hauser wears many hats: professional educator, wife, mother, and author. As a child on a farm in rural Indiana, Amanda led a life brimming with imaginative quests and romps across the midwestern countryside. She began writing at an early age and earned many scholastic awards before graduating with a bachelor of science degree in elementary education. She was the valedictorian of the class of 1998 at Saint Joseph's College in Rensselaer, and she went on to earn her master of education degree in curriculum and instruction at Indiana Wesleyan University. After spending nearly fifteen years in the elementary classroom, she developed a yearlong homeschool curriculum that immersed her children in various experiences across the entire United States. She and her husband are now busy raising their eight beautiful children in central Indiana, where Impish visits them each and every Christmastime.

CPSIA information can be obtained
at www.ICGtesting.com
Printed in the USA
BVHW020450140919

558413BV00002B/2/P